Paula Harrison

Tiara Friends

The Case of the Stolen Crown

SCHOLASTIC INC

For Alison Sellers,
my terrible twin

Chapter One

Cake Mixture

Millie stirred the cake batter so fast that the spoon flew around the bowl. She had to make sure there were no lumps. The cake was for her brother Prince Edward's first birthday and she wanted it to be perfect. Her arm started to ache, but she kept on stirring.

The mixture turned beautifully smooth and golden. A curl escaped from Millie's white bonnet and a drop of batter splattered onto her maid's apron. A cheerful fire warmed the palace kitchen. Shining saucepans hung on the wall, and there were shelves filled with pots of herbs and spices.

"Can I lick the spoon yet?" Jess danced around the table; her green satin dress swished as she twirled. Hop—step, step, spin. Her hair, tied up with a green velvet ribbon, bounced as she moved.

Millie smiled at her friend. "Soon! It's nearly done."

A plump woman with gray hair bustled out of the pantry. "There! That's all the deliveries put away." She wiped her hands on her apron and peered at the mixing bowl. "How are you doing with that mixture, Jess? Did you see the practice cake I made yesterday?" She pointed to a finished cake. "Looks like your fresh one will be even nicer."

The two girls exchanged looks.

"Yes, I think it's nearly ready." Millie smiled at Cook. "But actually, I'm not Jess. I'm Millie!"

Cook Walsh laughed and shook her head. "Of course it's you, Princess Amelia! You girls are such troublemakers for swapping places.

Be careful not to get caught!" She took the mixing bowl from Millie and gave it an extra stir.

"No one ever notices!" said Jess, twirling again. "I just went to Millie's ballroom-dancing lesson and Miss Parnell didn't suspect a thing."

Amelia (Millie for short) and Jess had been best friends ever since Jess became a maid at Peveril Palace three years ago. Jess's parents owned a dressmaking shop a few streets away. Jess's mother had made clothes for Millie since she was little and was well-respected at the palace. Jess had a bedroom near the kitchen where she stayed most of the week, going home to stay with her parents on her days off.

The two girls were born in the same month; although Millie always pointed out that she was ten days older. They both had glossy brown hair with hints of gold at the front. Their eyes were hazel, though Jess's were a little darker. They were exactly the same height. In fact, they were so similar that it was very hard to tell them apart.

Queen Belinda and Mary, Jess's mother, had found the likeness very handy. It meant Jess could do dress fittings for the princess's clothes while Millie was busy with other royal duties. But as soon as Jess tried on Millie's things, Millie wanted to try on Jess's. Since then, the two girls had swapped clothes more times than they could count and all without anyone (except Cook) finding out their secret.

Cook shook her head again. "Well, just be careful! What would the queen say if she saw you in that cap and apron? Now, let's get this practice cake out of the way and put your fresh one in the oven." She lifted the finished cake off the table and put it to the side.

"I like wearing Jess's uniform." Millie smoothed the white apron. "Especially if it means I get a chance to bake a cake!"

"And I like taking dance lessons." Jess did a pirouette. "Though I don't think I'd want to wear this dress *all* day long."

Cook Walsh smiled at them affectionately. "Who would have thought it? Peveril Palace has a maid that likes ballroom dancing and a princess that loves baking. The world is a funny place!"

The girls smiled back, their cheeks dimpling in exactly the same place and their hazel eyes sparkling.

"It's true!" said Jess. "We may look the same but we don't like the same things at all! C'mon, Millie. If you've finished baking I'd better teach you the new dance steps I learned. You'll need to know them for the party."

There were footsteps in the passageway.

"Cook Walsh, have you seen Princess Amelia?" called Queen Belinda. "I've been looking for her everywhere!"

Millie jumped and her bonnet fell off. She grabbed it and quickly crammed it back on her head. "Jess, what should we do?" she whispered.

"You have to act like you're me," hissed Jess. "I'll hide!" She dashed into the pantry and closed the door behind her.

The queen walked into the kitchen carrying Prince Edward. The little prince waved his chubby arms and gurgled. He was dressed in velvet breeches and a frilly white shirt. On top of his blond curls was a little golden crown sparkling with diamonds.

"Good morning, Your Majesty," said

Cook. "Oh, look at the little prince! How adorable he looks in his crown."

Millie, who was tidying the table when her mother came in, risked a quick look over her shoulder. Her baby brother did look sweet. She recognized the golden circlet on Edward's head. It was called the Baby Diamond Crown. It had been worn by each royal baby on their first birthday for hundreds of years.

Queen Belinda smiled. "Thank you, Cook! I wanted to put his party clothes on to make sure they fit. All the guests will want to see him wearing the Baby Diamond Crown. The queen gently stopped the baby prince from grabbing the crown and pulling it off. "If you see Amelia, could you tell her I need her upstairs straight away?" she continued. "I want her to try on her party clothes too. I think the dress may need some lace and beads to finish it off."

"I'll tell her, Your Majesty," replied Cook Walsh.

Millie pulled her cap lower as the queen swept past. Cook was right. Her mother would have quite a few things to say if she found out that Millie and Jess had swapped places. Queen Belinda could be very strict about royal rules and etiquette.

The pantry door opened a little and Jess peered around. "Is it safe?"

"She's gone! We'd better go and swap clothes again." Millie gave Cook a quick hug. "Thanks, Cook! I loved helping with the cake."

Cook smiled. "Off you go, now! And remember: Your mother wants you straight away."

Millie and Jess ran up the bare, wooden stairs to Millie's royal chamber. Millie wasn't really supposed to use the back stairs as they were for the servants, but it was quicker, and the brass railing on the first floor was perfect for sliding down.

There was no time for sliding this morning.

Jess and Millie took the left passageway leading to the royal chambers. Lanterns fixed to the wall cast a dim light over the corridor. Kings and queens with stern eyes stared down from dark paintings. Millie tried not to look at them too much. She started imagining they didn't approve of her wearing a maid's uniform. *Don't be silly*, she told herself, *they're just pictures!*

Another maid called Connie came out of a nearby chamber carrying a tray of cups and plates. She hardly glanced at the girls. Connie was three years older and thought she was super grown-up!

As Connie passed, there was a sharp click at the far end of the passage. A shadowy figure closed the door to the queen's chamber and ran away. In the darkness, Millie couldn't make out who it was. The figure vanished around the corner into the long gallery.

"Was that Mr. Steen?" whispered Jess. "I couldn't see."

Millie frowned. "I don't know." There was something strange about the way the person had scuttled away. Mr. Steen was the royal butler and liked to roam the palace giving out orders, but he didn't usually run around like that.

"If it was him, we should get out of here before he comes back," urged Jess. "He's bound to have a long list of jobs he wants me do to." She eyed Millie in the maid uniform. "Actually, he'll just give all the scrubbing and dusting to you!"

"That sounds even worse than Miss Parnell's dancing lessons!" Millie made a funny look of horror. "C'mon!" Grabbing Jess's hand, she dragged her along the corridor.

The girls dashed into Millie's chamber, quickly shut the door, and fell on the bed, giggling.

Chapter Two
The Little
Wooden Box

Millie and Jess laughed even harder when a golden cocker spaniel leaped onto the bed. His wagging tail thumped against Millie's knee.

"Jax, you're joining in!" Millie threw her arms around the dog. "I bet you want a walk, but I've got to try on my ball dress now."

"I'll take him," offered Jess. "We can go down to the lake. He likes it there."

She stroked Jax's floppy ears, which felt as soft as velvet. "Would you like that, boy?"

"Woof!" Jax thumped his tail even harder.

Jess pulled the ribbon from her hair and wriggled out of the green satin dress. "Ready to swap?"

"Ready!" Millie took off the maid's uniform and bonnet. Underneath, the girls wore cotton petticoats that looked like thin white dresses.

A large, round mirror decorated with carved, golden leaves hung on the wall. Millie glanced into the glass and smiled to see herself and Jess looking like twins—two girls in petticoats with glossy brown hair curling over their shoulders.

Then Jess pulled on her maid's uniform and tucked her hair beneath her cap. Millie fetched the pale-purple ball dress from her wardrobe and put it on.

Jess studied the fine dress. "Your mother's right. It needs lace and beads. We could buy some from Buttons and Bows."

Millie's eyes lit up at the mention of Jess's parents' shop. "That's a good idea! I'd love to go to Bodkin Street—" She broke off as she heard the queen calling. Her mother's voice sounded high and sharp.

Jess heard it too. "Something's wrong!" She opened the chamber door.

"I just can't find it anywhere!" the queen was saying. "I'm sure I put it right here."

Millie hurried to her mother's chamber with Jess right behind her. Prince Edward was sitting on the crimson bedspread, gurgling as he played with a little wooden horse. The queen dashed around him, looking under pillows and behind curtains. Her dark hair was escaping from its usually tidy knot and her cheeks were flushed.

Mr. Steen the butler stood beside the dressing table. "Are you *sure* you left it here, Your Majesty?" His eyebrows rose snootily. "You didn't put it back in the Royal Jewel Cabinet where it belongs?"

"No, no! At least I don't think so!" Queen Belinda lifted up Prince Edward to look underneath him before carefully putting him down again.

"Have you lost something?" asked Millie.

"Yes! Edward's little crown." The queen lifted the corner of the bedspread to peer underneath. "It has to be here somewhere!"

"Let me help, Your Majesty." Jess crouched down to look under the bed.

Millie began opening the dressing-table drawers.

"I'm sure I left it here on the dressing table," said Queen Belinda. "I took Edward into his room for a nap, but he didn't want to sleep. By the time I came back, the crown was gone!"

"Was anyone else here?" asked Millie, remembering the figure she'd seen in the passageway.

"No, I was alone." The queen smoothed her hair. "Maybe I did put it back in the cabinet . . . or maybe I left it downstairs! I did go to the kitchen and speak to Cook Walsh."

By now, more people had gathered in the doorway. There was Mr. Larum, a bearlike man with dark-rimmed glasses, who came to the palace three days a week to teach Millie science, history, and mathematics. Miss Parnell, the dance and deportment teacher, stood next to him, her high-heeled shoe tapping on the floor. The red scarf around her neck matched the red coloring on her lips.

Even Lord Chamberlain, the king and queen's most trusted adviser, had come to see what all the fuss was about. His long robe trailed along the floor. "Is everything all right, Your Majesty?" he quavered, resting on his cane.

"The Baby Diamond Crown has been misplaced," Mr. Steen told him. "We must begin a search for it immediately. Lord Chamberlain, would you check the Royal Jewel Cabinet, please? Remember we are looking for a small golden crown set with diamonds."

Lord Chamberlain bowed and hobbled away, his cane tapping as he went. Millie thought he accepted being ordered around by the butler very well.

"Miss Parnell, would you please check the kitchen, since Her Majesty was there earlier? Mr. Larum, please check the banquet hall and the parlor," continued Mr. Steen.

Miss Parnell's long ponytail swished as she spun around to leave. Mr. Larum lumbered after her.

"And Jess," Mr. Steen's voice grew sharper, "you must look in the prince's room and make sure you search thoroughly."

"Yes, sir." Jess hurried away.

"Oh dear! It'll be a terrible shame if Edward can't wear the Baby Diamond Crown at his party," said Queen Belinda. "For hundreds of years each royal baby has

worn that crown on their first birthday.
Everyone will notice!"

"We will make every effort to find it,
Your Majesty." Mr. Steen bowed and strutted
from the room. With his thin frame and
black suit, he always reminded Millie of a
strange, two-legged spider.

Millie helped her mother search the
bedroom all over again. Jax wandered into
the room and decided to help by tugging at
the bedspread. Prince Edward chuckled, his
rosy cheeks dimpling. Queen Belinda didn't
look quite so impressed.

"Sorry!" Millie caught hold of the
spaniel's collar. "He's getting restless. I'd
better take him for a walk." She pulled
Jax out of the door and dashed back to her
chamber to fetch his leash.

Before she took Jax for his walk, she
wanted to find Jess and talk things over.

The picture of the shadowy figure running away from her mother's room kept popping into her head. She wondered who it had been. Did they have anything to do with the missing crown? She quickly put on Jax's leash and hurried out along the gallery to find Jess.

The gallery was a long passage at the top of the grand staircase. It was lined with bookcases on one side. On the other side, a golden railing formed a barrier, and Millie leaned over it to get a perfect view of the entrance hall below.

Jess was standing, half-hidden, behind the cuckoo clock. Millie peered at her friend. What on earth was Jess doing? She looked as if she was hiding from someone.

The cuckoo clock on the wall near Jess began to chime and the cuckoo popped out to give its loud cry. The clock was deafening

and could be heard all over the palace, but Jess didn't even twitch.

Millie leaned over a little more, ignoring Jax, who was pulling on his leash. The only other person in the entrance hall was Mr. Steen, who was crouching down close to the massive front door. The butler was bending over a small wooden chest. As Millie watched, he closed the lid and turned a silver key in the lock. Picking up the chest, he hurried out of the palace, taking the steps two at a time.

Millie took in a sharp breath. Why wasn't Mr. Steen searching for the missing crown anymore, and where was he going with that little wooden box?

Chapter Three

Spying in Plumchester

Jess peered out from behind the door to the banquet hall and saw Mr. Steen disappearing down the palace steps. She dashed out of her hiding place, her black skirt swishing around her legs.

The door had closed behind the butler, but she heaved it open again. Mr. Steen was walking down the long cobbled driveway toward the golden gates at the entrance to the palace grounds. He'd left instead of helping search for the crown. Why?

She turned, hearing someone on the stairs, but it was only Millie with Jax. "Did you see that?" she demanded. "Mr. Steen went out, and he took a box with him."

"I can't believe he left when my brother's crown hasn't been found!" Millie gulped. "I'm starting to wonder . . . Do you think my mother really lost the crown, or do you think it was stolen?"

"I don't know." Jess bit her lip. "But I definitely saw Mr. Steen put something into that box before he left. We've got to find out what he's up to."

Millie's face dropped. "You'll have to go after him by yourself, Jess. I can't leave the palace grounds like this. Everyone in Plumchester will recognize me. Princesses aren't supposed to run around the town!"

Bored of standing still, Jax barked loudly and pulled on his leash. The girls shushed him.

"Here, let me take him!" Jess grabbed the spaniel's leash. "I've got an idea about how to disguise you. Come on!" She ran through the banquet hall and down the little passage that led to the kitchen, the laundry room, and the cellar.

There were voices coming from the kitchen. Turning to Millie, Jess put a finger to her lips, and she held her breath as they tiptoed past the kitchen door. She hoped Jax wouldn't make a sound. The door was slightly ajar, and Jess caught a glimpse of Miss Parnell and Cook Walsh.

Cook was scrubbing the table vigorously. "For sure, miss! The little prince's crown wasn't left in here. I would've seen it. Now, if you'll excuse me, I've got to get this cake into the oven." She picked up the baking tin filled with cake batter.

"I was only asking because the queen came in here earlier." Miss Parnell shook her head and sniffed. "If you're sure, I won't take up any more of your time."

"I *am* sure, and there was no need for you to go poking around while I was getting sugar from the pantry," Cook replied tartly. "I hope you haven't touched anything while I was out of the room."

Jess, Millie, and Jax ran into Jess's room at the end of the passage just in time. Millie closed the door softly, and they heard Miss Parnell marching away along the corridor.

"Take my oldest cloak and bonnet." Jess pulled them from her wardrobe. "No one will think you're the princess in these!"

"Thanks, Jess!" Millie put them on, wrapping the cloak over her ball dress and tying the bonnet string under her chin. The cloak had been patched several times and the bonnet string was frayed. They made Millie look very poor.

Jess put on another cloak and opened the chamber door a little. "It's all clear. C'mon, Jax! You'll get your walk at last."

The girls crept down the passageway and out the back door. Running across the stable yard, they took the path that led to the lake. Jess glanced back. The white-stone palace gleamed in the morning sun.

Jess, Millie, and Jax sped around a corner and the lake came into view. A playful breeze was chasing little white clouds across the sky and ruffling the surface of the water. The lake was wide at each end with a narrow stretch in the middle, spanned by a wooden bridge. Jess and Millie sometimes wished they could go out on the water, but the boats were always safely locked inside the wooden boathouse.

Jess glanced round quickly before dashing across the bridge with Millie and Jax close behind her. They ran up to a clump of bushes on the other side, and Jax's leash got tangled in the branches.

"Hold on! I can see where it's stuck." Millie took the leash from Jess and untangled it.

Beyond the bushes was a black iron fence that separated the palace grounds from the city of Plumchester. Jess ran her hand along the railings. She needed to find the loose one. Which one was it?

One of the railings tilted sideways. Jess moved it out of the way. "You and Jax go first," she told Millie.

Millie pushed the spaniel through the gap and squeezed through after him. Jess followed. Then they ran along a narrow lane and stopped at the corner of Peveril Street, the wide road that ran past the palace.

"There he is!" said Jess, spotting Mr. Steen's lanky figure in the distance. "Maybe he's heading for Halfpenny Square."

A horse and cart blocked their view for a moment. The girls crossed the street and hurried past a row of shops. They stopped at the entrance to a bustling market. This was Halfpenny Square, where the market traders of Plumchester came to sell their goods.

"Where is he?" Jess looked around. "I can't see him at all."

"Look! He's going into Emerald Alley." Millie pointed at the little side street. "He must be going to a jeweler's shop."

Jess's heart thudded. "Then maybe he really does have the crown in that box. He might be planning to sell it for a lot

of money. Quick—we're going to lose
him."

They pelted down the street, dodging fruit stalls and earning sharp words from a man taking cabbages off a cart. Stopping at the corner, they peered into the side street where Mr. Steen had turned.

Emerald Alley was a small lane with four jeweler's shops in a row. Mr. Steen disappeared into the shop on the end—Mr. Kinner's Fine Jewels. Millie and Jess ran to the window and peered in.

Inside were glass cabinets filled with gold watches, pearl necklaces, and diamond rings. Mr. Steen spoke to the shopkeeper, a small man with round spectacles, before coming out again. Jess and Millie ducked behind a wall to hide.

"You and Jax follow Mr. Steen," Jess whispered to Millie. "I'll go inside and find out if he sold that man the crown."

Millie nodded. "Be careful!"

Jess waited till the butler had walked into the next shop. Then, taking a deep breath, she went in. The shop was dimly lit, which made the jewelry look even more dazzling. A ruby necklace caught Jess's eye. It looked just as expensive as anything she'd seen at the palace.

"Yes, miss? Can I help you?" asked the shopkeeper. His forehead wrinkled as if he couldn't work out what she was doing there.

Jess was suddenly very aware of her plain cloak and bonnet. Maids didn't have enough money to buy expensive things like this. "Um . . . I just wondered . . . if it's not too much trouble . . . if you could tell me whether you have anything new to sell today."

"Anything new?" The jeweler's frown deepened.

"Yes, any new jewelry." Jess's cheeks flushed, but she carried on. "I'm really looking for a crown, actually. A small one."

"I don't have any crowns for sale." He glanced over Jess's shoulder. "What's going on, miss?"

Jess spun around. Millie was gesturing frantically from outside the window.

"Um, s-sorry," Jess stammered. "I have to go!" And she dashed out of the shop.

Millie caught hold of her arm, saying breathlessly, "You'll never believe it, Jess! I know what Mr. Steen said to the woman in the next shop. It was easy to hear because the window was open! He was asking her whether they could make another crown to replace the one that's lost. He took a drawing out of the chest and a bag of money."

"He's asking them if they can make another Baby Diamond Crown?" said Jess.

"Why is he trying to fix everything if he was the one who stole it?"

Millie's shoulders sank. Jax whined and licked her hand. "Maybe he isn't the thief after all. The trouble is, the jeweler told him it would take weeks to copy the drawing and make another crown, and the new one still wouldn't be as good." She blinked back tears. "What are we going to do, Jess? Edward can't go to his birthday party without the Baby Diamond Crown. Everyone's expecting to see him wearing it."

Jess was silent for a moment. She hated to see Millie so upset. "We should go back to the palace and search again. Maybe the thief left a clue behind when they took the crown. We can't give up. We just can't!"

Millie smiled faintly. "You're right! We've still got a whole day to find it." She held out her pinkie finger. "Double Trouble?"

Jess grinned. This was what she and Millie did when they'd decided something important together. It had begun when Cook called them The Doubles one day. Now it was a secret sign that only they knew. She linked her pinkie with Millie's. "Double Trouble!"

Chapter Four
Buttons and Bows

Jess and Millie hid behind a wall as Mr. Steen went into the last jeweler's shop. Jess's heart thumped as they waited for him to reappear. She hoped the royal butler wouldn't glance in their direction. They weren't very well hidden and she'd be in so much trouble if he saw her. Spying was scarier than she'd expected!

Mr. Steen came out a few minutes later. He left Emerald Alley with the wooden chest under his arm and a deep frown on his face.

"He doesn't look very happy, does he?" whispered Millie.

"Each of them must have said no to making a new crown," replied Jess.

Millie twisted the frayed bonnet string around her finger. "We should go back. Someone might notice we're gone."

Jess thought quickly. "Let's go to Buttons and Bows on the way. We can buy the lace for your ball dress. Then if anyone asks, we'll have a good excuse for being out of the palace."

The girls and Jax left Emerald Alley and walked up Bodkin Street. The crooked little lane was Jess's favorite place in Plumchester. She had lived here when she was very young, and she knew every shop, house, and cobblestone. She waved at Mr. Bibby, who was icing buns in his bakery, and smiled at Miss Clackton, who was cleaning the window of her pet emporium. She knew every shopkeeper was her friend—except Mr. Heddon in the hardware store, who wasn't very friendly to anyone.

The window of Buttons and Bows, Jess's parents' dressmaking shop, was hung with red and gold ribbons. In the center of the

display was a full-size mannequin wearing a dress of pale-blue silk with a long skirt trimmed with white lace. Jess's father would be out buying supplies of wool and cloth. It was always Jess's mother who minded the shop.

The bell jangled as the girls opened the door, and Mrs. Woolhead, Jess's mother, looked up from her needlework. "Hello, girls! I didn't expect to see you today. Look at you both!" She smiled fondly. "You look just as alike as ever." She looked more closely at Millie. "That's not one of your own cloaks though is it, Princess Amelia?"

"I borrowed it from Jess," Millie admitted.

Jess hugged her mom. "We came to get some decorations for Millie's party dress— maybe some lace and beads."

Mrs. Woolhead fussed over them, hanging up their cloaks. "Why don't you take that dog to the backyard and I'll find him something to eat."

A few minutes later, Jax was scarfing down some leftover sausages in the backyard while the girls were nibbling star-shaped gingerbread and drinking lemonade. Jess's mom solemnly listened to their story of the missing crown.

"So at first the queen thought she'd lost it," said Jess. "But we saw someone running away from her chamber, and the crown must be worth an awful lot of money."

"It's a sad day when someone steals from their own queen." Jess's mom shook her head. "It's never the people you'd expect either. Perhaps they'll be sorry and put it back."

"I hope they do," said Millie. "Every royal baby wears the Baby Diamond Crown at their first birthday party!"

"I remember you wearing it yourself," Mrs. Woolhead told Millie. "You looked adorable. Although when I visited the palace to finish sewing your special clothes, you kept handing the crown to Jess."

Millie and Jess looked at each other and grinned.

The dressmaker got out her measuring tape and a box of pins. "Now, let me see what I can do to make this party dress perfect."

Mrs. Woolhead was a fast needlewoman, and less than half an hour later, Millie's purple dress was trimmed with lace, and there were pretty flower-shaped beads across the top.

"Thanks so much, Mrs. Woolhead." Millie hugged the dressmaker before wrapping her cloak over her party dress again.

"You're welcome, Miss Amelia!" Jess's mom bundled up some extra lace and beads and put them in a parcel tied up with ribbon. "Take these extras just in case you need them. Now, you girls watch for carts when you're crossing the street."

Jess collected Jax from the backyard. The girls said good-bye before hurrying back to the loose railing in the palace fence.

"If the person that we saw running away from the queen's room really was the thief," said Jess thoughtfully, "then we know it can't have been Connie. She was right next to us at the time."

"We can rule out Cook Walsh too." Millie held the railing to one side for Jess to climb through. "She was in the kitchen when we went up the back stairs. She'd never make it up the other staircase before us."

"That's true!" Jess brightened. "Of course, we know Cook would never have done it anyway."

Pushing their way through the bushes, the girls reached the gardens. Ahead of them, the lake gleamed with the reflection of the tall white palace.

"Maybe, as well as looking for clues, we should see if anyone's acting suspiciously," suggested Millie.

"We can meet up tonight and compare what we've found out." Jess let Jax off the leash and the spaniel galloped straight into the lake. The ducks quacked angrily as Jax splashed around in the water.

"Oh, Jax! Now you'll need a bath," said Millie, laughing.

When Jess and Millie sneaked through the back door, they could hear Cook Walsh humming in the kitchen. Jax, who had been rinsed under the pump in the stable yard, settled down on a woolen rug by the laundry room where he often slept during the day.

"I'd better go upstairs. Mom might need me." Millie tucked the little parcel with the beads and lace under her arm. "I'll find you later."

Jess went into the kitchen just in time to see Cook taking the prince's birthday cake out of the oven. "That smells delicious!"

Cook Walsh set the freshly baked cake down on the table. It had risen perfectly and was a mouth-watering golden color. "Yes, it's come out well." She gazed at the cake and gave a huge sigh.

"What's wrong?" said Jess, alarmed.

"I just don't know if anyone will have the heart to eat any birthday cake tomorrow. Not with the little prince's crown going missing like this." Cook wiped her hands on her apron. "The whole palace has gone topsy-turvy and now people are whispering that it might have been taken on purpose. If I find out who took it I will give them a piece of my mind!"

Jess thought that if the thief saw Cook in one of her fierce moods, they'd definitely stay far away!

After Jess washed up the mixing bowl and spoon for Cook, she hurried upstairs with her feather duster. If anyone saw her, they'd think she was just doing her job, but really she would be searching for signs of the missing crown. If there were clues to discover, she would find them!

Chapter Five
The Footprint in the Gallery

Millie thought hard as she climbed the grand staircase. She was trying to remember what the dark figure running away from her mother's chamber had looked like. Had they been tall? Had they taken big strides or little steps? No matter how hard she tried, all she could remember was the swirl of their cloak as they rushed around the corner.

Of course, she didn't know for sure that the figure was the thief, but why else would they be running away?

Millie changed out of her party clothes into the green satin dress that Jess had borrowed earlier. She tied up her hair with a ribbon before going to knock on her mother's door. There was no answer, so she went to look in Edward's room. The queen was standing beside Edward's crib, watching him while he slept. She didn't turn around as Millie came in.

"I have beads and lace for my party dress now," said Millie. "It looks really nice." The queen still didn't turn around so she tried again. "Mother? Is everything all right?"

Queen Belinda tried to smile, but her eyes were sad. "Yes, darling! Could you watch Edward for a little while? I must speak to your father and Lord Chamberlain."

"Yes, I don't mind." Millie sat down beside Edward's crib.

As soon as her mother had left the room, Edward woke up and kicked his chubby little legs. Then he rolled onto his tummy and smiled at Millie.

"I suppose you want to come out." Millie lifted him out of the crib and gave him his little wooden horse. "How would you like to come and help me look for clues?"

Edward gurgled and chewed the ear of his toy.

"Good, that's settled!" Millie tucked him in the crook of her arm and crept up the passageway to her mother's chamber. Once inside, she set Edward down safely in the middle of the large four-poster bed.

Where should she start looking for clues? Her mother had said she'd left the crown on her dressing table, so it made sense to begin there.

Millie examined everything—her mother's perfume, hairbrushes, and face powder. Nothing looked odd or out of place. Finally, she looked under the bed, just in case the thief had dropped something by mistake.

Edward giggled and threw his wooden horse on the floor. Millie picked it up and made a funny face to make him laugh again. She gave him the horse back and sat down to think. Maybe if she found out where everyone was when the crown got stolen, that would prove who'd taken it. Whoever it was had to have been in the right place at exactly the right time!

Picking up Edward, Millie hurried out of the bedroom, down the corridor, and along the gallery. She took the stairs to the top floor of the palace and went into the schoolroom.

Mr. Larum was sitting at his desk, writing in a large leather-bound book. He looked at Millie over the top of his dark-rimmed glasses. "Princess Amelia, have you brought the little prince for a mathematics lesson?" He chuckled.

"Um, no!" Millie realized Mr. Larum was trying to be funny. She never really understood his jokes. "I just wanted to ask you something."

"I see. And what might that be?" said Mr. Larum.

Millie hesitated. Asking people where they were at a particular time might seem a bit strange and kind of nosy, but she really had to know. "I was wondering where you were this morning when the crown went missing." Her cheeks reddened. "I'm . . . um . . . trying to discover if anyone saw something that'll help us find it."

"A curious question!" Mr. Larum pushed his glasses on more firmly. "I'm afraid I didn't see anything at all. I was in my room reading a scientific encyclopedia when I heard raised voices. I opened my door, and there was Miss Parnell, also looking out of her chamber. We walked along the passage together to see what was amiss."

Millie held on to Edward firmly as he started to wriggle. "And you didn't see anyone else in the corridor?"

"No, indeed!" The teacher frowned. "And I do think you should leave these matters to the grown-ups, Princess Amelia. It is hardly suitable for you to roam the palace quizzing people!"

Millie stifled a sigh. If she only did *suitable* things, then she wouldn't have baked her brother's birthday cake that morning. It had been so much fun! Suitable things were hardly ever as nice as that.

She decided she'd better not say all that to Mr. Larum. "Sorry, Mr. Larum!" she said cheerfully.

"I suppose you meant no harm." Mr. Larum sniffed. "But this has been a most alarming day. After the crown disappeared, Mr. Steen ordered the guards to inspect everyone leaving the palace grounds. I went for a walk earlier and had my pockets thoroughly searched at the gate."

Millie tried not to giggle at his offended look. She was glad Mr. Steen had organized the searching though. It meant no one would be able to smuggle the stolen crown away from the palace. After all, no one else knew about the secret way through the fence except her and Jess. "Anyway, I think Edward might be hungry, so I'd better go," she told the teacher.

Mr. Larum rose from his chair and bowed. Millie noticed that his waistcoat had a large patch on the front and his shirt looked worn. As she hurried downstairs with Edward in her arms, she started wondering. Did Mr. Larum need money? He certainly hadn't bought new clothes for a while. Someone in desperate need of money might do a desperate thing . . .

It seemed horrible to suspect her teacher of taking the crown. He was a bit strange sometimes, but he'd always been nice to her.

Reaching the gallery, she found Mr. Steen and Miss Parnell staring at a dark patch on the floor. She dawdled, pretending to show Edward the books on the bookcase so she could listen to what they were saying.

"Could it have been made by one of the gardeners?" Miss Parnell was saying.

"It looks like a trail of muddy boot prints."

"No gardener has come upstairs today, and I made Connie wash this floor first thing this morning," snapped Mr. Steen. "Whoever left this mess came past recently."

"And the footprints are facing toward the stairs," said Miss Parnell, "as if the person who made them was running away. Maybe this will help us find the thief who took the baby's crown."

"I can only hope so," replied Mr. Steen. He and Miss Parnell continued down the stairs.

Millie stopped and stared at the muddy trail. It looked like whoever made them had quite big feet, so maybe they were a man's footprints. If Miss Parnell was right, these were the thief's footprints. This could be an important clue!

Checking that no one was looking, Millie set Edward down for a moment and took the ribbon from her hair. She held the ribbon close to the clearest footprint. Then, when she'd lined it up properly, she made a crease in the ribbon with her fingernail. She wanted to make sure she remembered how long the footprint was and, as she didn't have measuring tape, this seemed the easiest way to do it.

She gathered up Edward again. "We'll sort this out, don't you worry!" she whispered to him. "Jess and I are going to solve the mystery and get your crown back."

Chapter Six

A Disaster in the Dark

Jess had never seen so many gloomy faces as that afternoon when she went around the palace finishing her chores. She searched the upstairs chambers while she was supposed to be dusting, but she didn't find anything suspicious.

The only thing she discovered was a trail of muddy footprints on the gallery floor. As soon as the place was empty, Jess fetched a wooden spoon from the kitchen, measured one of the footprints, and marked its length on the spoon with a pencil. She wanted to remember how long it was in case it was a useful clue.

After supper, she crept up to Millie's chamber and knocked softly on the door before going in. Millie was sitting by the window in pajamas and a purple dressing gown embroidered with a golden crown. Jax was lying at the foot of the bed. His tail thumped drowsily as Jess came in, but he didn't open his eyes.

"I've been trying to work things out in my head, but they just keep getting more and more muddled," said Millie as Jess sat next to her on the window seat. "At least we know the crown is still here in the palace."

"How do we know that?" Jess demanded.

"As soon as the crown went missing, Mr. Steen ordered the guards to search everyone at the gate," explained Millie. "Mr. Larum told me. That means no one will have sneaked it out of here."

"OK, let's think about it. We know the person we saw rushing away from the queen's room can't have been Cook or Connie," said Jess, ticking them off on her fingers. "Connie walked past us just before, and Cook wouldn't have gotten upstairs fast enough. But that still leaves Mr. Larum, Miss Parnell, and Mr. Steen."

"And Lord Chamberlain," added Millie. "He was here too. Although he has been Lord Chamberlain since before my granddad died, so he doesn't seem the right sort of person to steal the crown. But remember how your mother said it's never the people you'd expect."

"None of them seem very likely." Jess frowned.

"I didn't find any clues in my mother's chamber, but I did measure a muddy footprint on the gallery floor." Millie took her hair ribbon out of her pocket. "I didn't have anything else, so I just measured it with this."

Jess grinned. "I measured it too—with this!" She took the wooden spoon out of her apron pocket and showed Millie the pencil mark on the end. "I reckon the only person with a shoe as big as this is Mr. Larum. Tomorrow we have to find a way to measure his shoes."

"That could be tricky because everyone will want to know what we're up to. Maybe it would be easier if we were in disguise!" Millie sprang up, her eyes gleaming. She twisted her hair into a bun before putting on a straw hat. Finally, she rummaged for some face paint and drew a false mustache above her lip in thick black lines. "What do you think?"

"Scary!" said Jess, smiling. "It doesn't *quite* go with the dressing gown."

Millie grinned. "OK, let me do your disguise next, and you're not allowed to look until I'm done."

Jess sat down with her back to the mirror. She had no idea what Millie would do. Millie loved jokes though, and would probably make her look as crazy as possible.

After painting Jess's face and trying on different scarves, Millie stood back and studied the result. She smiled broadly. "All right, you can look now."

Jess turned to the mirror and gasped. Her hair was tied in a high ponytail and a red scarf around her neck matched the red coloring on her lips. "Miss Parnell! You've made me look just like her."

Millie giggled. "Now you've just got to put on her high-and-mighty manner like this!" She stuck her chin in the air. "Show me your footwork for the waltz. No, Princess Amelia! Point your TOES! You look like a PENGUIN!"

Jess swirled around the room, pretending to do a perfect waltz. The cuckoo clock chimed downstairs and she grabbed hold of a bedpost to stop herself from twirling. "Eleven o'clock! Cook will scold me if she finds me up this late."

Millie got a hanky and handed it to Jess so she could wipe off the face paint. Then she rubbed off her own fake mustache. "Shall I meet you in the kitchen early tomorrow? We might not need the disguises." She cast a regretful look at the face paint.

Jess nodded. "We'll measure Mr. Larum's shoes and see if they look muddy." Jax jumped down from the bed and started scratching at the door. "Come on, Jax. I'll take you downstairs with me."

Quietly, she led Jax down the dark passage to the servants' stairs. The lanterns were unlit so she put one hand on the wall to steady herself. Moonlight shone through the narrow window at the end of the corridor and lit the way down the stairs.

"Are you thirsty?" Jess led the spaniel to the kitchen door. "Stay! Good boy!"

Jax sat obediently by the door.

Wishing she'd brought a lantern, Jess tiptoed inside. There was a dish in one of the cupboards that was used as Jax's water bowl. Hopefully, Cook would have put it back in its usual place.

Her foot nudged something, which rolled away across the floor, hitting the opposite wall with a loud clang. She froze. What if the noise had woken Cook?

Jax gave a low whine.

"Don't worry, boy." Jess took another step and her foot nudged something else. She bent down and groped around on the floor. Her fingers brushed against something smooth—a spoon. She picked it up. What on earth was going on?

Tiptoeing to the window, she opened the shutter. Moonlight streamed in, lighting the room. Jess gasped.

The whole kitchen looked like a disaster. Cups, bowls, and saucepans lay upside down on the ground. Flour was scattered across the floor and table. The birthday cake, which Millie had made so carefully, was torn open as if someone had taken huge handfuls out of it. The pots of herbs and spices had been opened and poured everywhere.

Jess stared at the mess and her stomach lurched. This couldn't have been an accident. Someone must have done it on purpose. It was really mean, especially ruining the cake. A person who would spoil a birthday cake must be absolutely horrible.

"Jessica Woolhead!" Cook Walsh stood in the doorway wearing her long green dressing gown and holding a lantern. "Oh my! Did that dog get loose in here?"

"No, it wasn't Jax, I promise! I just

brought him in for a drink of water. The room was already like this." Jess hoped Cook wouldn't notice that she wasn't in her night clothes.

"Oh my!" Cook repeated and sank onto a chair. "Perhaps it was a mouse . . . or a whole army of mice."

Jess gazed at the scattered spices, the ruined cake, and the flour all over the ground. She didn't understand. Suddenly, she noticed small round marks in the drifts of spilled flour. What had made those little circles? Were they made by the person who'd done this?

She whispered into Jax's ear. "Fetch Millie! Go!" She patted the spaniel and he ran away up the passage. Crouching down, Jess touched one of the marks. It was perfectly round and a bit bigger than the tip of her finger.

These marks were important somehow. But what did they mean?

Chapter Seven
The Marks in the Flour

As soon as she heard scratching at her door, Millie knew something was wrong. Opening it, she found Jax looking up at her with his deep, chocolatey-brown eyes.

"Hello, Jax. You shouldn't be up here. Where's Jess?" She tied her dressing gown more tightly and picked up her lantern. Jax followed her along the passageway, tail wagging. Millie heard voices as she came down the back stairs. Had Jess been caught sneaking to her chamber?

She was trying to think up excuses to help Jess out, when she stepped into the kitchen. Millie looked around, her heart sinking all the way to the floor. It looked like a storm had ripped through the room, throwing everything around. The bowls, the flour, the broken cake . . .

"Edward's cake!" she cried, rushing to the table. "What happened?"

Cook put a hand to her chest. "Princess Amelia! You made me jump. Now, don't you go worrying about the cake. That one is just the practice cake I made yesterday. The real cake that you made is locked safely in the cupboard." She took a bunch of keys from her dressing-gown pocket and unlocked the cupboard in the corner. Inside was the prince's birthday cake, resting on a silver plate.

"I'm so glad it's not ruined!" breathed Millie. "Oh, Cook! You're a genius thinking to lock it away."

"With something as precious as the little prince's birthday cake, I like to be careful." Cook's face was grim as she locked the cupboard again. "But I didn't think anything like this would happen. It's an absolute disgrace, that's what it is!" She got up. "I'm going to check all the outside doors. Maybe I can find out how the scoundrel got in."

As soon as she was gone, Jess whispered, "Millie, what if this has something to do with the missing crown?"

"Do you think it does?" said Millie, her eyes widening.

"Nothing like this has ever happened before," explained Jess. "And then it happens on the very same day the crown is stolen. It has to be connected!"

Millie wrinkled her brow. "I don't see how."

"I don't either, but I bet Cook comes back and says all the doors were locked. That'll mean this was done by someone here in the palace." Jess pointed at the round marks in the flour. "And look at these strange marks."

Jax licked at the flour and whined.

"Don't worry, boy!" Millie filled a bowl with water and put it outside in the passage. She rubbed Jax's coat as he drank.

Cook tottered back in. "Every single door is locked, so goodness knows how the varmint got in."

Millie and Jess exchanged looks.

"Oh dear, how my bones ache tonight!" Cook sighed. "And now I've got all this cleaning up to do."

"We'll clean up!" said Jess quickly. "You should go back to bed."

Cook looked doubtful. "You want to clean all this by yourselves?"

"We don't mind!" Millie told her.

"Well, I do have a big day tomorrow, what with all the banquet food to prepare," said Cook. "Thank you, girls! That's really kind."

When she was gone, Millie crouched down by the spilled flour. "It looks like someone stuck the end of a wooden spoon into the flour."

Jess knelt down and put a wooden spoon upside down into the mess. The spoon handle left a round mark, but it was smaller. "It's a different size."

Millie sighed. "It makes no sense! We'd better start cleaning up, I guess."

The girls began picking up the fallen saucepans and cups. Millie gathered up the ruined cake and then fetched a broom to sweep the floor.

Jess scooped up the spilled herbs and spices. She noticed that the pots of rosemary, thyme, and saffron were now almost empty. "Look how much was wasted!" she said, showing Millie.

"Your hands have turned a funny color," Millie pointed out.

"Bother!" Jess began scrubbing her orange hands with soap. "I forgot the saffron always stains my fingers."

Millie gazed at the freshly swept floor. A sudden idea made her head whirl. "You know what? Those round marks in the flour could have been made by a stick."

"A stick?" Jess stared.

"You know—a walking stick—just like the one Lord Chamberlain uses."

"But we were talking about Mr. Larum before. He's the only one with feet big enough to have made those footprints in the gallery."

Millie shook her head. "Maybe the footprints have nothing to do with Edward's crown. I didn't even notice them till after we'd come back from Emerald Alley, and that means they could have been made hours after the crown went missing."

Jess rubbed her forehead with stained orange fingers. "So the thief could be Mr. Larum with his big shoes or Lord Chamberlain with his walking stick."

"I guess so!" said Millie. "And if one of them *is* the thief, then they'll want to sneak the crown out of the palace. I think we should watch them really carefully tomorrow."

Millie woke up late the next morning, tired out by all the excitement of the night before. Her heart sank as she remembered that today was Edward's party. This afternoon, lots of important lords and ladies would be arriving, and the Baby Diamond Crown was still missing. She sprang out of bed. She'd better get dressed!

Millie went down to breakfast and gave Edward a hug. "Happy birthday, little brother!"

Edward gurgled and waved his jam-covered toast.

He was the only one at the breakfast table who looked happy. Millie's father, King James, was eating a pastry with a deep frown on his face.

Queen Belinda was pale, and there were shadows under her eyes. She offered Millie some toast. "Amelia, would you set out the place cards on the banquet table before everyone arrives? I have so many other things to do!"

"Yes, I can do it!" Millie took the bundle of place cards and the toast.

"Oh, and Miss Parnell wants you to go straight to the hall after breakfast for one more dancing lesson," added her mother.

Millie stifled a groan. She was about to ask if she could skip the dancing when Mr. Larum came in, followed by Jess.

"I do apologize for appearing at breakfast dressed so oddly," Mr. Larum told the queen, pointing at his tweed slippers. "But one of my shoes has gone missing. It's very strange indeed."

Millie looked at Jess. She knew her friend was thinking the same: It was very suspicious that Mr. Larum's shoe had disappeared just when they wanted to measure it.

"I suppose there could be a shoe thief as well as a crown thief in our midst." Mr. Larum tried to laugh, but stopped when he saw the queen's serious face.

Jess whispered in Millie's ear as she passed by with a tray. "You keep an eye on Lord Chamberlain, and I'll follow Mr. Larum."

Millie nodded, her mouth full of toast. She finished her breakfast quickly. She hoped to set the place cards out on the banquet table and go looking for Lord Chamberlain, but Miss Parnell pounced on her as soon as she reached the banquet hall.

"Princess Amelia, I hope you are ready to shine on the dance floor?" Miss Parnell arched one eyebrow. She was already wearing her party dress, which was made from peach-colored silk, along with high-heeled shoes and white satin gloves.

Millie was suddenly aware how messy her hair was (because she hadn't brushed it), and that she had jam on her dress from hugging Edward.

Lord Chamberlain came in, leaning heavily on his stick, and began instructing some grooms from the stables about where to hang the streamers.

Millie tried to hear what he was saying. If Lord Chamberlain had hidden the crown, where would it be? It seemed wrong to suspect him when he was so old and so hard-working!

"Are you listening, Amelia?" Miss Parnell

put her hands on her hips. "Remember to point your toes while you waltz. Show me your steps now, please, and then we must practice the fox-trot as well." She clapped out a rhythm. "One, two, three, one, two, three . . ."

Millie began to twirl. She saw Lord Chamberlain leave in the direction of the kitchen. Why was he going that way? Her mind whirled faster than her feet. If only Miss Parnell would let her go. She had a missing crown to find, and she was running out of time.

Chapter Eight
Two Princesses

As soon as Miss Parnell let her go, Millie dashed to the banquet table and hurriedly set out the place cards. The hall looked amazing. Silver-and-gold garlands hung from the ceiling. The long table was set with white china plates and crystal glasses. Mr. Steen was busy sweeping the dance floor and, at the far end of the hall, an orchestra was unpacking their instruments.

After getting rid of the place cards, Millie

rushed down the passageway to the kitchen. She hoped to find Lord Chamberlain, but instead she ran into Jess carrying a tray of melon slices.

"Oops!" Jess steadied the tray. "Millie! I thought you'd be changed by now. The party starts in less than an hour!"

The cuckoo clock in the entrance hall chimed one o'clock, as if to prove Jess's point.

"Miss Parnell made me practice dancing all this time!" Millie gasped. "I'm exhausted! And I couldn't follow Lord Chamberlain and I know he came this way."

"I lost track of Mr. Larum too," admitted Jess. "I followed him halfway around the croquet lawn, into the stables, and past the fountains. He's been wandering around a lot, but he might just be looking for his missing shoe."

"I can't keep an eye on both of them at the party AND waltz perfectly at the same time," said Millie. "My feet ache already!"

"If Cook had let me serve at the banquet table, I'd be there to help you," said Jess. "But she's told Connie to do the serving. She says I should take a rest because of all the cleaning up we did last night."

"Then you're free to do whatever you want!" Millie's eyes gleamed. "I've just had the most amazing idea!"

"What's that?" Jess stared. "It's not something silly, is it?"

Millie smiled mysteriously. "I'll show you! Can you come right now?"

"I suppose." Jess left the tray of melon in the kitchen where Cook was adding the final decorations to Edward's enormous birthday cake.

The cake was covered with glittering

pale-blue icing. On the top there were little animals—a horse, a lion, a duck, and many more—all made from icing too.

Millie felt a swoop of excitement when she saw how lovely it was. "That looks beautiful!" She hugged Cook Walsh. "Do you need any help?"

"No, I've nearly finished. Then it'll be ready to go behind the curtain in the banquet hall. It'll be a nice surprise for the king and queen, and little Prince Edward!" Cook smiled. "Go on now; you've got a party to get dressed for!"

Millie and Jess dashed up the back stairs.

"What's your idea?" said Jess as they reached the top.

Millie shook her head, glancing at Mr. Steen, who had just emerged from the linen closet with a pile of napkins. They hurried into Millie's chamber and closed the door. Jax, who was sleeping on the bed, woke up and gave a soft bark.

"Tell me quick!" Jess fixed her gaze on Millie.

"Well . . . as soon as the banquet finishes, there'll be dancing in the hall," said Millie. "My mother will take Edward into the parlor to open his birthday presents. There'll be a chocolate fountain in there too."

"So?" Jess prodded.

"There'll be guests everywhere and whoever's stolen the crown could try to sneak it out of the palace while things are busy. So . . . it would be easier if there were two of me!"

"You think I should dress up like you?" Jess's eyes widened. "But people will notice that there are two princesses!"

"Not if we stay in different places! You stay in the banquet hall—you're better at dancing anyway—and I'll keep watch in the parlor and the drawing room." Millie went to her wardrobe and pulled out two long purple dresses. One was her party dress, all decorated with lace and beads. The other was quite plain. "The only thing is, we have to make this dress look the same as the party one and we have less than an hour to do it."

"We can do it!" cried Jess. "Where's that spare lace and the beads?"

The girls got a needle each. Jess quickly sewed some lace on to the plain dress, while Millie attached the beads. When Millie had sewn the last bead, they held the two dresses next to each other.

"That's pretty good!" Jess pointed at the newly decorated dress. "Although this one is a darker mauve and the lace isn't sewn so neatly."

"I bet no one but your mother would notice the difference." Millie changed dresses and fastened her hair into a high knot, while letting some ringlets hang loose. "Let's wear gold necklaces too."

Jess pulled on the other party dress and fastened her hair to look the same. Then she

stood still while Millie placed the gold chain around her neck. They put on gold tiaras sprinkled with little purple amethyst jewels. Finally, Millie picked out two beautiful bracelets with matching charms. She fastened the crown charm on her own wrist and the dress charm around Millie's.

"How does that look?" Millie stood by Jess's side. They were nearly identical except for Jess's eyes, which were a deeper hazel, and her dress, which was a little darker.

"This dress is so beautiful!" Jess pulled the long sleeves over her hands. "I just hope no one notices my orange fingers. I've washed my hands over and over, but the saffron color won't come off!"

"I'm sure no one will see it." Millie put on some purple satin dancing shoes and gave a second pair to Jess. "I should go downstairs.

The guests will arrive soon."

"Wait! We need a signal," said Jess. "In case one of us sees someone sneaking away with the crown."

"We can set off the cuckoo clock in the entrance hall," said Millie. "It's so loud we'll definitely hear it over the sound of the orchestra."

"Good idea!" Jess grinned. They'd played a game where they set off the cuckoo clock when they were younger. All you had to do was move the big hand till it pointed at twelve and the clock would chime. The little bird would come out of its door and cuckoo several times. Millie and Jess had loved it, but the queen had gotten a little tired of the game and told them not to do it anymore.

Hearing the clatter of hooves and carriage wheels, Millie glanced out the window. There was already a procession of carriages rolling down the palace drive. Jax pricked up his ears. Then his tail drooped and he leaped off the bedspread and dived under the bed.

"Poor Jax!" Jess kneeled down. Reaching under the bed, she stroked him. "You've never liked noise and visitors, have you?"

"I'd better go!" Millie straightened her tiara and headed for the door. "You could stay in the gallery till the banquet is over. As soon as the dancing starts, I'll give you a thumbs-up."

"I'll be ready. But, Millie?" Jess's face was serious. "Don't try to stop the thief on your own. They could be dangerous."

Millie held out her pinkie and Jess linked it with her own. "Don't worry. I'll find you and we'll stop the thief together. We're Double Trouble!"

Chapter Nine

Jess's Ballroom Dance

Jess hung back in a dark corner of the gallery and watched the guests arrive. The lords wore velvet cloaks and hats, while the ladies had pearl necklaces and sparkling rings. King James stood at the door to greet each guest. Jess couldn't see Millie, Queen Belinda, or little Edward. She guessed they must have already sat down at the banquet table.

Edging closer to the balustrade, she saw Lord Chamberlain walk across the entrance hall, leaning on his stick. Mr. Larum and Miss Parnell followed, both dressed in their best clothes. Jess's heart beat faster. Lord Chamberlain's stick looked just the right size to make those marks they'd seen in the flour last night. But why would he mess the kitchen up like that? It didn't make any sense!

The guests made their way into the banquet hall for dinner, and the orchestra began playing soft music. There was the sound of knives and forks on plates and glasses clinking. With no one to spy on, Jess decided to practice the steps Miss Parnell had taught her when she'd taken Millie's dancing lessons.

At last, the sounds of the banquet grew quieter. A few people wandered through the main entrance, and the orchestra struck up a lively tune. Mr. Larum came out of the banquet hall and headed toward the outer door. Jess stiffened. Was he leaving the palace? She sighed in relief as he swung around and went back into the hall again.

A moment later, Millie skipped past. Glancing up at the gallery, she gave a secret little thumbs-up. Jess's stomach tumbled over. It was time for her to play her part! As soon as Millie disappeared into the parlor, she hurried down the stairs and into the banquet hall.

The room was a whirl of music and color. Ladies waltzed across the dance floor, their skirts flying out as they spun. People gathered at the tables, talking and sipping glasses of wine. Jess's breath stuck in her throat. She'd never been in a room with so many lords and ladies before.

A lady dressed in bright yellow held out
her hand. "How lovely to see you, Princess
Amelia!"

Jess gulped. "Um, lovely to see you too!"
She shook the woman's hand before hurrying
toward the dance floor. At least if she was
dancing, no one could insist on talking to her!

As she skirted past a table, she overheard Mr. Larum. He was talking to a bald gentleman. "So I found my lost shoe in the center of the maze. I've no idea how it got there. Of course, some people like practical jokes, but I do hope they won't use my footwear for their amusement next time."

Jess thought his face looked completely truthful. A sudden thought dropped into her head: Maybe someone else had taken Mr. Larum's shoe. They'd used it to make the muddy footprints in the gallery and then hidden it afterward. Maybe they had wanted to make the footprints look like a clue when it wasn't at all.

Jess was wondering who would be horrible enough to do that, when she noticed movement in the corner of the hall. There was an alcove near the orchestra that was completely hidden by a long red curtain. The red drapes bulged and Cook's elbow and skirt poked out at the side.

Jess smiled. She knew what Cook was up to! This was where Prince Edward's first birthday cake was being hidden. Just before they sang "Happy Birthday" to the prince, the curtain would be pulled back to reveal the surprise.

"Princess Amelia!" said Miss Parnell sharply. "I thought I'd see you dancing, not shuffling around the hall like this."

Jess was so busy staring at the quivering red curtain, that she forgot for a moment she was supposed to be Millie.

"Princess!" snapped Miss Parnell. "Are you listening? I'd like to introduce you to Lord Deller as a suitable dance partner." She beckoned to a young boy in a shiny green tunic.

"Oh, thank you!" When Jess saw that the boy was half her size, she had to stop herself from giggling. "Um, nice to meet you, Lord Deller."

"Call me Tom! Would you give me the honor of a dance?" squeaked the boy, holding out his hand.

Jess snorted with laughter, but managed to turn it into a cough. She took Tom's hand. As he whirled her onto the dance floor she reminded herself that she was here to keep an eye on anyone who might have stolen the crown. Over there she could see

Mr. Larum and Miss Parnell. Lord Chamberlain was sitting at the back of the hall. She couldn't see Mr. Steen, but she hoped he was in the parlor where Millie was watching out for anything suspicious.

Getting her dance steps right and keeping an eye on the suspects took up all of Jess's attention. She curtsied to Tom at the end of the dance, saying, "I'm a little thirsty now, so I'm going to get a drink."

There was a table at the side where Connie was serving fruit juice. Forgetting how long her skirt was, Jess tripped over the hem just as she reached the table. She stumbled and bumped into Miss Parnell, who had just collected a glass of elderflower juice. The juice splashed out of the glass all over the tablecloth and Miss Parnell's white satin gloves.

"Darn it! Silly child!" hissed Miss Parnell, before seeming to remember that she was speaking to a princess. She gave a fake smile. "Well, accidents will happen, I suppose."

"I'm really sorry." Jess bit her lip. Miss Parnell's satin gloves looked very damp. "Would you like me to fetch a napkin?"

"No, no! Just leave it." Miss Parnell sighed, pulling off her left glove and giving it a shake.

Jess was about to offer to fetch the dancing teacher a fresh pair of gloves, but her words dried up in her throat. She stared at Miss Parnell's hand. The tips of her fingers were orange. The bright color was unmistakable. It was the color of saffron.

Jess looked from her own stained fingers

to Miss Parnell's. She knew the dancing teacher must have made all the mess in the kitchen the night before.

Her gaze traveled down to Miss Parnell's feet. Of course—the high heels! They would make little round marks in the spilled flour just as well as Lord Chamberlain's stick.

Did this mean Miss Parnell had taken the Baby Diamond Crown?

The teacher noticed her sudden silence and glanced at her suspiciously. Then, pulling her glove back on, she walked away with what was left of her glass of fruit juice.

Jess stared after her. She was sure the mess in the kitchen and the missing crown were connected. She had to tell Millie about this! She dashed out the banquet hall into the main entrance, nearly colliding with a bearded man who was examining his reflection in the hall mirror.

Her fingers trembled as she turned the big hand on the cuckoo clock to the next hour—four o'clock. The clock chimed at once. Jess dashed up the stairs with the cuckoo's call ringing out behind her.

Chapter Ten

The Surprise Behind the Curtain

Millie jumped when she heard the cuckoo clock ring out. The king and queen were chatting to a lady with a rose in her hair. Edward was sitting on the floor playing with his favorite new present—a brightly painted spinning top. Mr. Steen was standing beside the refreshments table as if he were guarding the chocolate fountain.

Millie had heard the guests mutter as

soon as they saw Edward without the Baby Diamond Crown. Her mother was trying to smile, but Millie could tell from her pale cheeks that she still felt sad.

Hearing the clock chime, she ran out into the entrance hall. Where was Jess?

"Goodness gracious! There she is again!" mumbled a bearded man by the mirror. "I thought she went up the stairs."

Millie knew he must be talking about Jess. Hurrying upstairs, she found her friend in the corner of the gallery. "What did you see?" she asked breathlessly.

Jess told her about the orange stain on Miss Parnell's fingers.

Millie's heart sank. "What if she hid Edward's crown in the kitchen last night?"

Jess frowned. "But why leave such a mess? It only gives it all away. There must be something else going on."

"I'll go and watch her," said Millie. "We can't both go in there dressed like this."

"I'll put my maid things on." Jess ran along the gallery to the back stairs. "I'll be as quick as I can!"

Millie knew something was happening as she entered the banquet hall. People were murmuring in excitement and Mr. Steen was calling for quiet. The king and queen were at the front with the butler. Edward was in Queen Belinda's arms. Millie scanned the room for Miss Parnell.

"Quiet please, everyone," Mr. Steen repeated, placing his hand on the long red curtain.

Millie smiled. They were about to reveal the cake and sing "Happy Birthday" to Edward! She was sure her little brother would love his gorgeous cake.

But where was Miss Parnell?

"Amelia!" King James spotted his daughter. "Come and join us, my dear."

Millie made her way to the front. She still couldn't see Miss Parnell. Had the dancing teacher disappeared on purpose?

Her mother leaned forward to kiss Edward's golden curls. "Wait till you see this, my darling."

"Now we're ready," boomed the king. "Pull back the curtain, Steen."

With a ceremonial air, the royal butler grasped the red curtain with both hands and drew it back.

There was a gasp, followed by silence.

The birthday cake was gone.

Everyone started talking at once. Mr. Steen searched behind the curtain. Queen Belinda covered her mouth with her hand.

"Where's Cook?" bellowed King James. "Someone fetch Cook Walsh!"

"I don't believe it!" cried the queen. "First Edward's crown and now this!"

Millie dashed for the door. She had to find Cook. She nearly ran straight into Jess, whose maid dress was wonky and whose hair was falling out of her bonnet.

"I saw what happened!" gasped Jess. "But Cook left the cake right there. I saw her do it!"

"Someone's taken it, then." Millie blinked back tears. "How could they?"

"Because they're a mean, nasty little person. That's why!" growled Jess. "But they can't have run away very fast with a huge cake like that!" She raced toward the kitchen corridor.

"Wait, Jess!" cried Millie. "We don't know which way they went."

"That's true! I'll check the kitchen and the back stairs. You go the other way!" Jess dashed off again.

Millie stopped and tried to think. Voices were growing louder in the banquet hall. The entrance could be crowded with guests at any moment. Where had the thief gone with the cake, and why?

Maybe they wanted to eat it all themself. That seemed strange since it was such an enormous cake, but maybe they were very hungry. Anyway, they'd definitely want to go somewhere quiet.

"Did anyone come past with a cake?" she asked the guard at the front door.

"No, Your Highness," said the guard.

Millie twisted her necklace. Where would the thief go? Quickly, she made up her mind. Crossing the hallway, she opened the door labeled STATE ROOM and slipped through.

In the center of the room was a large oval table stacked with paper. Her father's cloak was slung over one of the chairs. This was the room where her parents talked to Lord Chamberlain and other advisers about everything that was going on in the kingdom of Lavania. Millie wasn't usually allowed to come in, but there was no one here to complain.

Tiptoeing through the room, she listened at the next door, which led to her father's study. It sounded as if there was someone moving on the other side. Holding her breath, she opened the door a little.

The room was empty. The papers on the king's desk were rustling in the breeze blowing through an open window.

Millie crossed to the next door which led to the Royal Library. Was Jess having more luck in the kitchen? What if the thief had gone upstairs? No one was checking up there.

The library was empty too. Sunlight glinted on a thousand specks of dust floating above the vast bookcases. Millie hurried across the polished floor, making the dust swirl. There was just the Crimson Room left—a room with a large fireplace and soft, red sofas. It was the room the queen liked to use in winter when it was cold.

She thrust the door open and froze. Her hand tightened on the doorknob.

Miss Parnell was standing over Edward's birthday cake with a long, sharp knife. Her orange-stained fingers gripped the knife handle and a look of determination gleamed in her eyes.

Slowly, she brought the knife down until it hung just above the sparkling blue icing.

Chapter Eleven
A Glint of Gold

Millie's insides turned cold as she saw Miss Parnell plunge the knife into the icing. "Stop it! Why have you stolen the cake?"

Miss Parnell looked up in surprise and her face darkened. "Stolen the cake!" She pretended to laugh. "Don't be silly, Princess Amelia! I'm just cutting it into slices for the guests. Go back to the banquet hall and I'll be along in a moment."

"You shouldn't have taken it away!"

Millie's voice trembled. "And where's my brother's crown? Did you take that too?"

"Don't be ridiculous! I don't know anything about the missing crown." Miss Parnell put down the knife and picked up the massive cake. Her eyes darted to the outer door that led into the courtyard.

"Millie! Where are you?" Jess called.

Her voice was faint. Millie knew she must be several rooms away. "I'm in the Crimson Room!" she called back. "Come quickly! I found the cake."

There was the sound of a door slamming and footsteps.

Miss Parnell tried to hold the cake with one hand while she opened the outer door. The cake wobbled dangerously and an icing duck fell to the floor.

Jess burst in from the library. "You said

you'd found the . . . oh!" She stared at the dance teacher.

"On three, we grab the cake," Millie muttered out of the side of her mouth. "One, two, three!"

Jess and Millie dived opposite ways around the red sofa. Miss Parnell slammed the cake back on the table and snatched up the knife. "Stay back!" she screeched. "I'm keeping this cake."

"What's going on here?" King James came through the library door carrying Prince Edward. Queen Belinda and Mr. Steen followed him. "Miss Parnell, why is the prince's birthday cake here? It was meant to be in the banquet hall."

Miss Parnell put down the knife and glued a smile to her face. "Oh, Your Majesty! I'm sorry if you were worried. Princess Amelia and Jess were playing with the cake and being a bit careless, I'm afraid, so Cook Walsh asked me to take it somewhere quiet to cut it into slices for the guests."

Millie's cheeks reddened. How dare she?

A white-aproned figure appeared behind the King. Cook Walsh waved her wooden spoon at Miss Parnell. "I said no such thing! Your Majesty, I never asked her to take the cake anywhere."

Miss Parnell shrank back. "Well, I did it for the best, I'm sure. Now, if you excuse me, I'll finish up here and bring the cake to the banquet hall in a moment." Her fingers brushed the sparkling blue icing.

Suddenly, Millie felt the clues fall into place.

She remembered the figure running away from her mother's room. She remembered Mr. Steen sending everyone to look for the crown. She knew for certain that Miss Parnell had been told to search in the kitchen.

"We'd only just finished mixing the cake," she muttered to herself. "That's when she went down there."

Jess shot her a questioning glance. Widening her eyes, Millie jerked her head toward the cake. A look of understanding spread across her friend's face.

"At least the cake's been found," said Queen Belinda. "We can tell our guests. They'll be so happy after the disappointment about Edward's crown."

"You're right, my dear," King James said to the queen. "Let's return to our guests and let them know that all is well. Miss Parnell, please bring the cake back to the banquet hall. We'll await you there. I'm sure you had good intentions in moving it, even though it was a little foolish."

The queen took the king's arm and they turned to walk away.

"No, wait!" shouted Millie.

"There's one more surprise!" Jess picked up the cake knife before Miss Parnell could reach it.

"Amelia!" cried Queen Belinda. "What *is* this all about?"

"Everything's been so busy," began Millie, "that we never told you how someone messed up the kitchen last night."

Miss Parnell's hands twitched and she clasped them tightly.

"That's true!" Cook nodded. "It was a huge mess!"

"One of the things that got spoiled was Cook's practice birthday cake," Millie told them. "It was broken from top to bottom. Of course, the person that spoiled it didn't know it was the practice one. Did you, Miss Parnell?"

"Don't be ridiculous, Princess Amelia!

You shouldn't talk such nonsense in front of everyone." Miss Parnell's eyes flicked back to the birthday cake.

Jess leaned closer to the sparkly blue icing. "The top of this cake is quite bumpy. See that lump there, right next to the elephant?"

"I did my best!" said Cook. "The top of the cake came out very uneven. It's never really happened before!"

"I know why the cake is bumpy," Millie told her. "You see, there's something inside that's not supposed to be there!"

"Let's show them," said Jess.

Millie held the cake steady while Jess sliced gently down the middle. The knife clinked as it met something hard. There was a glint of gold in the middle and the sparkle of diamonds.

"The Baby Diamond Crown!" cried the

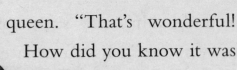

queen. "That's wonderful! How did you know it was in there?"

Millie nodded at Miss Parnell. "She must have taken it from your room, but then Mr. Steen wanted the whole palace searched. So, when she was sent to check the kitchen, she dropped the crown inside the cake batter. No one would think to look in there! The cake went into the oven with the crown inside it, and it's been there ever since!"

"You wicked woman!" Cook shook her wooden spoon at the dance teacher again. "I should've known you were up to something—sniffing around my kitchen like that."

"And that's why Miss Parnell made the kitchen so dirty last night," added Millie. "She hoped to get the stolen crown out of the cake, but when she couldn't, she messed up everything so that no one would guess what was going on."

"But her fingers got stained with saffron, just like mine did when I cleaned up the spices later." Jess pointed from her own orange fingers to Miss Parnell's.

"Guards!" bellowed the king. "Remove Miss Parnell from the palace immediately."

A guard dressed in a red uniform marched in and led the dance teacher through the courtyard door. Miss Parnell muttered something about horrible princesses and nasty maids, and cast a sulky look at the king as she was taken away.

Surprised by his father's loud voice, Edward began to cry.

Cook took an icing sheep from the top of the cake and gave it to him. "Don't worry, dearie! Cook will get your crown out of there and put the cake back together, easy as pie! But first, we're going to sing you 'Happy Birthday'!"

Edward stopped crying and gave Cook a smile. "Happee Burday!" he gurgled, before putting the icing sheep in his mouth.

Chapter Twelve
A Special Treat

After everyone sang "Happy Birthday," Cook took the crown out of the cake and cleaned off all the crumbs. Queen Belinda placed it on the prince's head and the diamonds shone brightly on the band of gold.

King James, who was

still holding Edward, smiled broadly. "You did some excellent detective work finding the crown, girls. It certainly deserves a treat. Name anything you would like. Anything at all!"

Queen Belinda's eyebrows rose. "Are you sure, my dear? Anything?"

"Of course! They're sensible girls, I'm sure," said the king.

Jess and Millie looked at each other. Jess's heart skipped a beat. A chance to do whatever they liked! It might be a long time till the grown-ups were as kind as this again. Even Mr. Steen was nodding and smiling at them!

Millie whispered in Jess's ear. "How about the lake?"

"I was thinking that too!" cried Jess.

They turned to the king and said together, "We'd like to go rowing on the lake, please!"

"Excellent!" said the king. "Mr. Steen will open the boathouse for you."

"Just make sure you're careful climbing in and out of the boat," said the queen.

Cook Walsh brought the cake to the kitchen and put it back together using a little extra icing. The king, queen, and most of the guests crowded around the table to watch. Jess and Millie helped with the final touches. Jess squeezed some sugary icing from the piping bag, and Millie molded it into a flower before sticking it over the last crack on the top of the cake.

Cook smoothed away the last dab of icing. "There we are!"

"It looks as good as new!" said Queen Belinda. "Thank you, Cook Walsh! You really are amazing."

"I had some very good helpers." Cook smiled at Jess and Millie.

Mr. Steen gathered up the cake. "I shall set this in its place of honor in the banquet hall, Your Majesties."

"Thank you, Mr. Steen!" said Queen Belinda. "Now, you must all come and join the party. Cook and Jess—I absolutely insist that you come and enjoy yourselves!"

Later that afternoon, the girls took a rowboat out on the palace lake. Jess trailed her fingers through the water. "This is great—I wish we could take a boat out every day."

"It's brilliant!" Millie pulled hard on the oars. "Isn't it, Jax?"

Jax gave a sharp bark. He was sitting in the prow of the little rowing boat. His eyes were bright, and the breeze ruffled his coat.

"The best thing is, with Miss Parnell gone, there'll be no more dancing lessons until they find a new teacher," said Millie.

Jess grinned. "Not that you went to many of the lessons."

"I let you teach me the steps afterward," protested Millie. "I would *much* rather be baking with Cook Walsh though. It was so funny when she shook her wooden spoon at Miss Parnell. I thought she was going to rap her on the head!"

"Cook is quite fierce sometimes! Here, shall I have another go?" Jess took the oars and rowed a little before stopping to let a family of ducks paddle by. Jax barked at them, as if to hurry them along.

"I think you were amazing to realize where Miss Parnell had hidden the crown," Jess told Millie. "She thought she'd tricked everyone."

"You spotted her orange fingers," said Millie. "I think we were a pretty good team!"

"We should try some more mystery

solving." Jess nodded toward the shore where Mr. Steen was serving strawberries and cream to the guests. "See that lady in the pink hat with the golden feather? What if she was actually an acrobat in disguise? See how she's tapping her foot as if she wants to get up and perform?"

Millie giggled, noticing the strange bulges underneath her friend's bonnet. "I'm not sure about that, but I can see a mystery right here that needs solving. The mystery of the lumpy cap!" She leaned forward and pulled off Jess's cap.

"Huh?" Jess clutched at her head. She was still wearing the amethyst tiara from earlier. It gleamed brightly in the sunshine. "Oh! I changed back into my maid's clothes so fast, I must've forgotten to take it off!"

"No wonder it was making such a lumpy shape under your cap. I'm glad we're matching again." Millie touched her own tiara before holding out her pinkie.

Jess grinned as she linked fingers. "We're Double Trouble!"

Time to Decorate!

Can you help Cook Walsh get ready for the party by decorating Prince Edward's birthday cake?

You could add stars, jewels, flowers, and a crown!

Spot the Difference

Can you spot the 5 differences?

Hidden Gems

Can you find the six hidden gems within this word search?

T	P	G	L	H	S	J	D	F	F
P	B	A	E	G	E	A	N	K	S
D	I	A	M	O	N	D	Z	P	A
H	A	E	E	P	X	E	I	W	P
K	Q	M	R	T	D	U	R	H	P
T	D	X	A	B	P	I	Z	D	H
R	S	I	L	W	V	E	J	A	I
M	U	K	D	Q	X	R	A	I	R
A	T	B	H	B	S	E	V	R	E
Z	J	F	Y	T	G	L	O	T	L

★ Diamond   ★ Emerald   ★ Jade

★ Sapphire   ★ Pearl   ★ Ruby

Paula Harrison is a bestselling children's author, with worldwide sales of over one million copies. Her books include The Rescue Princesses series. She wanted to be a writer from a young age, but spent many happy years being an elementary school teacher first.

Visit her website
www.paulaharrison.jimdo.com

Welcome to the
ENCHANTED PONY ACADEMY,
where dreams sparkle and magic shines!

ENCHANTED PONY ACADEMY

All That Glitters

Lisa Ann Scott

■SCHOLASTIC

ENCHANTED PONY ACADEMY

Wings That Shine

Lisa Ann Scott

■SCHOLASTIC

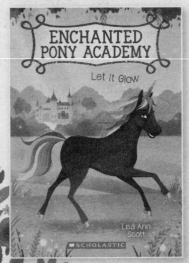

ENCHANTED PONY ACADEMY

Let It Glow

Lisa Ann Scott

■SCHOLASTIC

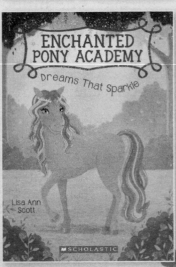

ENCHANTED PONY ACADEMY

Dreams That Sparkle

Lisa Ann Scott

RAINBOW magic

Which Magical Fairies Have You Met?

- ❑ The Rainbow Fairies
- ❑ The Weather Fairies
- ❑ The Jewel Fairies
- ❑ The Pet Fairies
- ❑ The Sports Fairies
- ❑ The Ocean Fairies
- ❑ The Princess Fairies
- ❑ The Superstar Fairies
- ❑ The Fashion Fairies
- ❑ The Sugar & Spice Fairies
- ❑ The Earth Fairies
- ❑ The Magical Crafts Fairies
- ❑ The Baby Animal Rescue Fairies
- ❑ The Fairy Tale Fairies
- ❑ The School Day Fairies
- ❑ The Storybook Fairies
- ❑ The Friendship Fairies

◼ SCHOLASTIC

Find all of your favorite fairy friends at
scholastic.com/rainbowmagic

HiT entertainment

RMFAIRY17

Visit Friendship Forest, where animals can talk and magic exists!

Meet best friends Jess and Lily and their adorable animal pals in this enchanting series from the creator of Rainbow Magic!

SCHOLASTIC

scholastic.com

MAGICAF10